YEARNING FOR THE SEA

Additional World Literature in Translation Published by Frayed Edge Press:

Ere the Cock Crows
Jens Bjørneboe; translated from the Norwegian by Esther Greenleaf Mürer
Includes a reconstruction of the original play by the translator.

Winter in Bellapalma
Jens Bjørneboe; translated from the Norwegian by Esther Greenleaf Mürer

Full Fare
Jean-Bernard Pouy; translated from the French by Carolyn Gates, Jean-Philippe Gury, and Robert Helms

YEARNING FOR THE SEA

Esther Seligson

Translated by Selma Marks

Frayed Edge Press
Philadelphia, PA

Originally published as
Sed de Mar, por Esther Seligson
Artífice Ediciones, Primera Edición, 1987

Translation @Selma Marks, 2020
1st English Language Edition
Published by Frayed Edge Press, 2021
With the kind permission of Geney Beltrán Félix

https://www.frayededgepress.com/
This book is printed on acid-free paper

Cover image ©Rogelio Cuéllar
Used with his kind permission

Publishers Cataloging-in-Publication Data

Names: Seligson, Esther 1941-2010. Sed de mar. | Marks, Selma, translator.
Title: Yearning for the sea / Esther Seligson ; translated by Selma Marks.
Description: Philadelphia, PA : Frayed Edge Press, 2021. | Summary: Picks up
    the story of Homer's Odyssey at the point of Ulysses' return to his wife Penelope,
    twenty years after the destruction of Troy, with an emphasis on Penelope's
    feelings of loss and desire.
Identifiers: LCCN 2021930889 | ISBN 9781642510331 (pbk.) | ISBN
    9781642510348 (ebook)
Subjects: LCSH: Homer.--Odyssey--Adaptations--Fiction. | Man-woman
    relationships--Fiction. | Odysseus, --King of Ithaca (Mythological character)--
    Fiction. | Penelope--(Greek mythological character)--Fiction. | BISAC: FICTION
    / Fairy Tales, Folk Tales, Legends & Mythology. | FICTION / Family Life /
    Marriage & Divorce. | FICTION / Feminist.
Classification: LCC PQ7298.29.E5 S4413 2021| DDC 863 S45--dc23
LC record available at https://lccn.loc.gov/2021930889

CONTENTS

Introduction

Naomi Lindstrom

Esther Seligson was a poet, novelist, playwright, literary critic, occultist, and teacher. She was born on October 25, 1941 into an observant Jewish family in Mexico City and lived her life in the Mexican capital, except for often lengthy stretches of time spent in France, Israel, India, Tibet, Portugal, and elsewhere. Seligson was something of a cult author whose allusive work was most highly valued by readers with a sound general education. While she never attained wide popularity, she was greatly respected by other writers, and her work won the Xavier Villaurrutia Prize and the Magda Donato Award. Her essays appeared in such Mexico City outlets as *Plural*, *Diálogos*, and *Vuelta*, magazines of general intellectual interest, as well as the more academic *Revista de la UNAM*. A translator and popularizer of both literary texts and philosophical writings, she was especially known for her dissemination in Spanish of the work of the Romanian-born philosopher and essayist Emil Cioran. Seligson was one of the Spanish-language translators of the literary production of the Egyptian-French Jewish writer Edmond Jabès.

Seligson stood out for her wide-ranging erudition as well as for her creative talent. She began her undergraduate work in chemistry at the Universidad Nacional Autónoma de México, but soon left the sciences to finish her degree with concentrations in Spanish and French literature. Seligson went on to complete a master's degree in art history at the Instituto de Cultura Superior, and then took further graduate courses in history and philosophy at the Sorbonne and the Université de Bordeaux. As she became more concerned with strengthening her Jewish learning, she pursued coursework at the Centre Universitaire d'Études Juives in Paris and the Pardes Institute of Jewish Studies in Israel.

Over the course of her career, Seligson taught courses at numerous institutions all over Mexico City on a very wide variety of topics including theater production, the history of theater, medieval art, comparative religion, mythology, and Jewish thought and mysticism, as well as literature. She was a pillar of the Mexico City theater scene, a stalwart supporter of university theater, and at the time of her death was the weekly drama critic for the newspaper *Proceso*. Especially in her mature years, she devoted considerable time to mentoring emerging writers and other creative people; her critiques have been described as both pitilessly unsparing and, in the long term, beneficial. For a time she ran a weekly salon for younger talents in her Mexico City apartment. Seligson, who had been suffering from heart trouble, went into a fatal cardiac arrest on February 8, 2010. She is buried in the Panteón Israelita in Mexico City.

From her earliest appearance on the cultural scene, Seligson stood out for her mystical outlook, both in literature and in life generally. She was a serious student and practitioner of astrology, an expert Tarot reader, and well versed in the healing and talismanic properties attributed to various stones; she told, using various systems of divination, the fortunes of her friends and followers. Seligson was generally seen in long, flowing skirts and tunics and wearing memorable jewelry that took the shape of a scorpion, a reference to her astrological sign, or held some other symbolic significance. She developed a sui generis spiritual system that became increasingly syncretic over time as her knowledge expanded. Readers of her literary writing may easily surmise that she possessed a thorough knowledge of the great Catholic mystic writers who are central figures of sixteenth-century Spanish literature, especially San Juan de la Cruz, as well as an acquaintance with Kabbalah. During a South Asian journey, she adopted the philosophy and practices of Tibetan Buddhism and this current of thought infused itself into her writing and daily life. While Seligson's writing is at times soaringly abstract, it could also be intimate and personal. The 2004 *Simiente* (*Seed*) deals with the suicide of one of her two sons, the actor Adrián Joskowicz. *Seed* is a hybrid text that includes passages from Adrián's personal journals, letters, and Seligson's poems. It constitutes, among other things, a memorial to Adrián and some honest observations from Seligson about her feelings, experiences, and behavior as a mother.

Her literary work makes evident the importance that she gave to the great mythic tales of humankind. She is especially known for the 1981 *Morada en el tiempo* (*Dwelling in Time*) and the present work, titled in the original Spanish *Sed de mar* (1987) and translated by Selma Marks as *Yearning for the Sea*. These two long stories constitute new versions of tales from the great sources of the Western narrative tradition: Jewish history, narrative, and thought (*Dwelling*) and the mythology of classical antiquity (*Yearning*). *Dwelling in Time* is a reworking, in poetic prose, of the story of the Jewish people. It follows the mythic and historical record from the creation of the universe to the Holocaust and its aftereffects, compressed into 118 pages. This singular text is richly allusive; it draws upon the Hebrew Bible, the Talmud, the writings of the first-century Roman-Jewish historian Josephus, and many other historical and literary sources up to the mid twentieth century. Dwelling emphasizes supernatural episodes, such as miracles, visions, and prophecies, over the patriarchal themes of land claims, battles, military campaigns, and numerous descendants. *Yearning for the Sea* is essentially a refashioning of selected portions of the *Odyssey*.

In Seligson's variant of the epic tale, Penelope and her prolonged wait for Ulysses's return, which is given a surprising outcome, become the main focus. Ulysses's travels recede into the background while Penelope emerges as the heroine of a story of a woman seeking, among other things, self-determination. In this account, her husband is notable mostly for stranding his wife on the Greek mainland, aching with loneliness and unfulfilled desire, while he dallies at length on the islands with Circe and Calypso. As readers quickly discover in a preamble composed by the couple's son Telemachus, his mother did not possess the unquestioning and inexhaustible loyalty that Homer attributes to Penelope. After losing patience with "enslaving herself to the wait," as Ulysses's old wet nurse Eurycleia puts it, she has abandoned Ulysses, apparently quite shortly before he could arrive back in Ithaca. After reading Penelope's goodbye message, the

Homeric hero is astonished by his wife's bold move and left unable to carry out the dramatic scenes of recognition and reunion in which his epic voyage is supposed to culminate. Yet, as Penelope observes in the letter, she knows that he will not pursue her even if he knows where to find her.

Telemachus serves as the fictitious editor of the text of *Yearning for the Sea*. Some time after both his parents' deaths, he has gained access to Penelope's diary and her farewell letter to Ulysses, which he offers to readers with a warning that her writings contain unexplained gaps and might have been censored by Eurycleia out of "her need to preserve Penelope's image as mother and wife." He also includes in his volume texts in the voices of Eurycleia and Ulysses in which they provide their takes on Penelope's departure. Eurycleia was originally brought into the household to be Ulysses's wet nurse, but she appears to have transferred her loyalty from her master to the bereft woman of the house, and has become her trusted companion, sympathizer, and spokesperson. She defends her mistress's decision to flee Ithaca. Addressing Ulysses and speaking on behalf of all women, she states the case bluntly: "Our mistake is to have waited so long and to have anxiously come out to meet you as if your ship had really hastened to reach the mainland. But in fact it is being held back by one obstacle: you driving your banner in, claiming us women as property and fastening us to the shore." The ancient nurse is the character through whom feminist thought is most clearly articulated in *Yearning*.

In her diary and her farewell letter, Penelope eloquently expresses the reasons for her unhappiness in Ithaca: the lack of any outlet for her sexual desire, which she describes as intense, and the misery of weaving and waiting while her husband is roaming all over the Mediterranean and happily falling victim to love spells. In her letter to Ulysses, the last text in the collection, she expresses the disillusionment that she experienced in her assigned role and her growing realization that, while Ulysses dominated her thoughts, she was barely present in his: "The most difficult thing, Ulysses, was to accept a clear and simple fact: that you stopped loving me, that you began to forget me, to feel comfortable with the absence, like lying on a secure and soft bed…" She envies Ulysses the freedom of his adventures on the islands and has inwardly recreated his escapades with Calypso, featuring herself in her imagination as the protagonist. Despite its apparent frankness, Penelope's account leaves much still veiled.

Readers know that Penelope has fled Ithaca, but to where and what has she escaped? In the "Epilogue" to *Yearning*, Telemachus transcribes Penelope's farewell letter. Far from resolving the unknowns surrounding the events of the plot, in the manner of the epilogue to a conventional nineteenth-century novel, the final segment multiplies them. At the outset of her letter, Penelope refers to her destination as the Island of Everlasting Time. This mysterious locale has few identifying characteristics, and does not seem to be an island in the same sense as the Aeaea where Circe kept Ulysses in a state of enchantment or Calypso's Ogygia; it seems as much a state of mind as a geographical feature.

The chief attraction that the Island of Everlasting Time holds for Penelope is the possibility that it will offer her a zone free from Ulysses, even if some things remain unchanged: "I keep weaving exactly as I have woven myself. There is one difference, however. Here there is not even a trace of you so I am free to invent everything—I left so many remembrances tied to my loom, so many loose threads—beginning with my own destiny." Though she declares herself free of her husband, she is addressing to him a lengthy letter full of memories of scenes from their marriage and the years that she spent awaiting his return. In Penelope's outlook, the mysterious Island of Everlasting Time also holds out the promise of liberation from what has hitherto been her self: "Penelope is no more, she has been left behind." She feels compelled to give a reason for her decision to flee to the Island, and her explanation generates further mystery. Dismissing such mundane reasons as dislike of domestic chores, she elucidates her choice by stating that one night she "felt the touch of the call" and knew that the time had come to make her move. At the end of the letter, and of Seligson's narrative, in lieu of any concluding statement readers find two unanswerable questions "The silence—tell me Ulysses— does it speak? What does silence say when it is silent?"

Yearning is exceptional for several reasons. Penelope's diaries and letter, the most vivid segments of the text, offer some well realized passages in which sexual desire is expressed from the perspective of a woman. The narrative as a whole exemplifies Seligson's ability to rework ancient narratives for her contemporary readers, modernizing the thematic material without the use of anachronisms. I hope that Selma Marks's able translation will provide English-language readers a point of entry into the complex and extensive literary universe of Esther Seligson.

Austin, Texas
December, 2020

Translator's Note

Selma Marks

Those of us who have read Homer's Odyssey (and many who have not) are aware of the basic outline of the plot: Ulysses, king of Ithaca, abandons his queen Penelope and his newborn son Telemachus to fulfill his warring duties in the Greek war against Troy. He returns to Penelope twenty years later, after the destruction of Troy and his long voyage back home, delayed by various obstacles that the gods have thrown in his way. Penelope has been waiting for him, resisting the demands of her many suitors to re-marry. For years she works on weaving a mantle, saying that when it is finished she will choose a husband—but at night she secretly unweaves it. When her ruse is discovered, the pressure to marry again mounts. Just then Ulysses arrives home and, helped by his son who is now a young man, he kills the pretenders and re-unites with Penelope.

The myth of Ulysses and Penelope presents a prototype of the relationship between a man and a woman joined in a socially sanctioned sexual bond: marriage. Its central theme is fidelity. In *Yearning for the Sea*, Esther Seligson delves into that theme, asking herself: What did this separation mean to this man and this woman who loved each other in the flower of their youth and who, after struggling against all odds, are now re-encountering each other marked by the long separation? This is the portal through which Seligson enters into a confessional world of the senses, of the feelings of sexual desire, of love and its absence, of loneliness, of the overwhelming nostalgia for past times and bygone youth that the separation of this man and this woman evoked in her.

Her version is a re-interpretation of the myth in the modern terms of a woman who lived in the second half of the twentieth century, and who was shaped by the issues of the day—both in Mexico, where she was born (1941) and studied, and in her life abroad in France and Israel where she lived for many years pursuing her interests—her "passions," as she called them—in philosophy, mythology, and various religions. But Seligson does not recur to the myth as a mere ploy to put forward her modern conceptions. She takes the myth seriously, incorporating and even brandishing its central elements as the core of her own re-interpretation.

Thus, as in the myth, her Penelope and Ulysses live in a harmonic relationship, a man and a woman united in conjugal bond and each excelling in the performance of the functions socially allotted to their sex: Penelope in charge of reproduction, and caring for the household's daily needs; Ulysses the ruler of the household and the kingdom, the dispenser of law, the warrior and citizen. And, as in the myth, that harmonic relationship lives within the hierarchical context of male dominance: Seligson's Penelope lives under the protection and guidance of Ulysses. She is defined by him; her life and her identity are reflections of her relationship to her husband, as wife and as mother of his child. Like all virtuous women of classical thought, she is morally and physically dependent, and cannot take significant action without the supervision of her guardian. She lives virtuously secluded behind the household walls; her universe is confined there.

But Penelope changes after Ulysses leaves. In the myth, that change comes about when, provoked by her suitors' behavior, she is forced to make the decision, on her own, about whether or not to re-marry. Hers is a complex decision that goes to the essence of the issue of fidelity posed in the myth: she has to choose between her own personal desire to remain faithful to Ulysses, and her obligation, as his wife, to protect his estate from the suitors who for years have been eating his food and drinking his wine, and protect his line of descent from their threat to kill his son Telemachus. By taking an independent moral stand she becomes a protagonist, a leading figure on her own right, thus joining the other female protagonists of Greek antiquity such as Clytemnestra, Antigone, and Electra. Like them, she turns into an agent, a catalyzer of a confrontation—in her case it is an indirect one, manipulative and behind the scenes—that causes a temporal "break" in the established patriarchal order. This challenges the male-dominated classical conception of women as empty vessels defined by their male guardians. But as in the case of her sister heroines, her status as protagonist is short-lived and only ends in the re-affirmation of the patriarchal order, in her case by subsuming herself into her role as Ulysses' wife and mother of his son.

Seligson's Penelope changes, too. But unlike the mythical Penelope, her change is directly triggered by the absence of Ulysses himself, specifically by his having abandoned her. And she is less troubled by her social obligations to defend her husband's estate and descendance than by the impact of his leaving on their personal relationship, particularly their intimate sexual relationship. In contrast to the mythical Penelope and the other classical female protagonists, Seligson's Penelope follows a path of her own personal desires. She unravels the thread of those desires, which the myth mentions but never unwinds from their spool, and in doing so, begins to redefine herself in her own terms, apart and separate from her husband. In this way she closes off the possibility of re-entering and re-affirming the patriarchal world she comes from. She ends alone, isolated, on the Island of Everlasting Time.

Seligson's Penelope is, in that sense, a modern woman. Yet, the very means she relies on to become one, to make the voyage towards her own identity, are drawn from Greek mythology itself. Classical, male-dominated thought not only divides male from female in terms of social tasks, but also regards them as embodying profoundly different principles, with different ways of relating to the world. The male principle is wound up around considerations of honor in war, and is based on the rationality of the law, of the *polis*, and its rights and obligations. The female principle is characterized by a logic of desire, of unbound feelings, sensuality, and passion. These two principles are seen as antagonistic, mutually exclusive. The feminine can potentially destroy civilization—the *polis* and its laws— founded on male rationality. It is dangerous and therefore must be subdued and tamed. That is why women are institutionally subordinated to the male order through patriarchal marriage and patrilinear succession, and are segregated into the confines of their home, their "true nature" hidden, buried, kept silent.

Seligson focuses on the suppressed feminine of classical mythology and brings it to the fore, reclaiming a place for the world of the senses, of passion, of sexual desire. It is by entering into that realm that she and her Penelope arrive at an understanding of themselves. Engaging with that mythical feminine of the senses is thus a valid, legitimate means to acquire knowledge, especially self-knowledge. And it is an equally valid means to know and understand the "otherness" of the "other," of Ulysses, of the male. Homing in on what the myth suggests about Ulysses' nostalgia for his country, his hearth, his son—a nostalgia so intense that it moves Athena to petition Zeus to remove the obstacles against his return to Ithaca—Seligson extends the feminine principle to the male world as well. By approaching men on that basis, she and her Penelope are able to understand them, and thus gain a better understanding of themselves: "To allow oneself into the gaze of the other makes me become the other in relation to myself and walk towards the re-creation of the human being as a totality."

It is that world of the senses, of desire and passion, that form the matrix from which Seligson proceeds to articulate, or, as she would say, "to name" the unspoken, the unwritten. The more she approaches it with her profoundly expressive, carnal, and visceral language, the more alive it becomes.

New York City
December, 2020

There will surely arrive a presence to quench your thirst
Maybe this absence that keeps imbibing you will go away
—*Cuarto solo.* Alejandra Pizarnik

I am thirsty.
For water?
Made with slumber? No,
with morning dawn.
—*Sleepless Suite.* Xavier Villaurrutia

I
Preface

I found these papers in a locked casket that my father kept in his rooms. They are fragments of Penelope's diary, which were preserved, in turn, by Eurycleia, his loyal nursemaid, the same one who transcribed and annotated—possibly in order to relate it to my mother—Ulysses's shock when he found he had been abandoned by the woman who had waited for him for twenty years. The letter Penelope sent to him arrived torn up, for the messenger was attacked and robbed as soon as he disembarked to carry out his mission. Yet there was no lack of people who, aware of the fate of the letter, and willing to offer their services to the great Ulysses—either because they knew him personally, or in order to obtain a reward, or simply impelled by a desire to add some adventure to their routine—took on the task of recovering parts of what was lost. Regarding the diary's fragments, Eurycleia was never able to explain the omissions and ellipses. I have wondered if she took matters into her own hands and censored out what might have offended Ulysses, or that clashed with her need to preserve Penelope's image as mother and wife.

In accordance with tradition, I, Telemachus, laid a lock of my hair on each of their graves, poured out milk and honey to quench the thirst of their tombstones, and prayed for their souls to meet again in the Meadow of the Asphodels so they don't suffer the fate of those buried bodies, so far away from each other…

II
PENELOPE

An image, I am running after an image whose name I cannot find, I am running after a name with letters I don't recognize, unpronounceable letters, and I need to talk to you, Ulysses, to talk to you in order to know if the time that I invented for myself is real, if it is true that the waiting is over or if I have only fallen into another hopeless parenthesis, if I have only become entangled with words for not having hearkened to my own, for listening to them only inside me, for not embodying them, boneless whirls of mist dispersed by my own breath… To talk, yes, to recover that dialog that does not need explanations to explain itself, the fabric woven with the threads of the little everyday things that pile up amid the silences and that burst out into words, like prisms coming into contact with a light beam, opening up, acquiring color… To talk of what I don't have, of what I don't know how to say and that once I have said it allows me to receive, and learn, and touch, bashful, to talk of these my breasts rising towards you, still full of awe and yearning for life, for the green, for the sea, for that sea you have been traversing, leaving behind my body wrapped in the memory of your last caress—a memory soon to become my shroud, fragments of a dream bursting in the middle of my vigil, lacerating my skin, sentries on permanent watch waiting for the signal, that game between the waiting and the fear that the waiting is over; fear yes, of your face, different and unknown to me, marked by unspeakable visions tempered in lands that are to me nonexistent, heavy with the dew of the many eyes that must have watched you depart during those sunrise leave-takings. And your body, what new caresses shall I use to let out its rushing laughter and be certain that it does not overflow with yearning for a more discerning touch? Fear that our embrace will crumble like clay between my fingers, that its scent will end up being confused with the cold of the night, just like the blackened vehemence of the sheet on which we made love that bygone afternoon, our last one… I no longer want to keep track of time, of that time that so long ago we stole from Time to consecrate it to our love, I don't want to walk down the strands of my memory and wear off, one by one, our encounters, yellowed pearls… In the beginning everything was rage, a thick hazy anxiety at the center of my womb deprived of crown and scepter, rummaging through our bed hunting for your presence, walking back and forth from the hill to the port to see if, preyed upon by the same hunger, you had turned around your ship's bow. And I would scream myself into fits of drowning fury, and curse Destiny with the bitter resentments of a widow, and fight against your parting like someone fighting a demon who, mocking me, ended up endearing itself to this, my appalled and rebelling body. I would then howl, my hands destroying the weaving shuttle once and a thousand times over, and dream to compel the remembrance: after having been taken in your arms—I would tell myself—would another's arms know how to hold me? While in my sitting room my Suitors' lust exhaled its web of mirages ensnaring me from head to toe, I would whisper in front of the mirror "take me, take me into the luminous hollow of your embrace and welcome my passionate surrender, everlasting"… Fiercely, I would recreate our embraces, one after the other, the damp spasms, and then fall, exhausted, in thrall of my demon. I will tell you what my dreams were like, Ulysses: a slow-acting poison, a poison that made that extraordinary moment bloom, a voice climbing up my throat, born from the earth's silence, searching for the fruit and announcing the imminence of its pleasure, a shout pounding in my breast and seeping, feverishly, back into my blood; how can I let it out now that you have left me to the mercy of empty days, barren and burning with desire, alone by myself? Not to have an image of myself anymore, not to know who, or what, or where I was going. I grieved your absence to the limit of my endurance, listening to it pacing through my veins, slowly, holding me captive, tormenting my flesh, withering my thoughts. And yes, the time for love was time stolen from Time, a theft that must be paid back, the Gods demand it mercilessly. It is not as if I did not know that everything comes to an end. In fact, that is how I was brought up, to never forget that at the end of our mortal life nothing remains of our beauty and pleasure but dust, ashes and dust, and of our desires and deeds only a faint acrid scent, short-lived too, transient creatures, rudderless travelers that invariably end up boarding Charon's boat as the only certainty of having walked on this earth. But I also heard talk about famous lovers being rescued, and believed that you would force open the doors of the Netherworld, that the intensity of my urge for you would have impelled us both to lend our names to a star. What madness and how it lulled me! I devoutly trusted in its power, I fed it in my breast like a virgin impregnated by a celestial breath… Meanwhile you fled, engrossed in your wartime duties, forgetting, forgetting me… I can feel you, Ulysses, I can feel you. The voyage of desire that brings you closer begins where the sea that separates us ends, the flight of a thousand birds like islands over the water softly landing on it, and then everything becomes a bridge, the vineyards ripening on the slopes, the call of the turtledove, the solitude of the shepherd, the bareness of the tree, the smell of bread, the nursery rhymes, and all of the light is your presence inside me… Wash me, wash away with your hands the sadness of my body and the sadness of my face, dust of orphanhood accumulated in my long wandering gaze searching for you, falling asleep in the afternoon in some strange place, a solitary refuge without your arms to shelter it that little by little, from hope to dejection and dejection to hope begins to crack and then explodes… My voice is silenced by the humbling plea, desire blushes… With time, the time for love turns into a sacrilege, and that demands reparation. I was not prepared, I confess, I did not imagine it would demand so much in exchange and so unhurriedly proceed to methodically extract its justice: this much I gave you and this much I am taking. And how much it gave! And how generously! And I, thinking I deserved everything, the euphoria, our embraces, the myriad iridescent shells in the hollows of your kisses, every awakening culminating in a bounty of roses, wonders of light in each transition to the climax, and receiving, welcoming the whole universe into each cell, the joy, the cherished dialog between the intimate and the profound... To talk, yes, I need to talk with you, Ulysses, to know if I am just inventing it or if it was true, if in your soul still swirls a similar whirlwind, if your hours have been similarly wasted, if in some fold of your memory floats something like a phantasmagoric boat prodding and softly taking you towards the hope of the re-encounter... To talk, to say, perhaps, that what is not real is this waiting, that what is frozen inside me is not these seeds still longing to sprout, and that what stretches out before us is not the irremediable ocean. And I shudder, I shudder for the words that have not been said, for the hardening of their silvery flow, for the persistence with which the wheel of Nemesis keeps swallowing the helpless buds, I shiver with fear for our faith in the efficacy of a dialog fed by absences, for into whose ears have you been spilling our wedding chants each day more distant?... Whose lips now keep the record of all your battles, of your victories won in the quest we both forged?... I had forgotten you are a man of spare words, Ulysses, that you barely express your feelings, that we have never received news directly from you, that your son is growing without having seen your face, without having heard your voice. Trapped in an indecipherable sign, spellbound by a flame spinning around and consuming me, drop by drop, my thoughts wither and I grow wan, every exit has been getting narrower, the warp of the fabric that I weave in the morning and that I unravel at night will soon turn into a rag, unraveled threads full of emptiness where I will end up crumbling... Too many moons have passed since I last called for you or felt outraged; one could say that the debt has been satisfied and that its rodent's gnawing has burrowed through to the marrow of my bones, for there is no net that can hold me up. And yet, from time to time a Poet comes around, and when his strings sing your heroic deeds, a new furrow opens up in my body. In the beginning it was all fire, the breath of your breath drawing me in until sated without respite between expectation and bliss. It is my voice that impels him, I would tell myself—the force of his arrows glimmers with the golden halo of his desire to return quickly, the shield that protects him has my name engraved on it, he is coming, he is coming, unquestionably overpowering every obstacle... But you took your time, Ulysses, and your delay began to gather its own momentum, to rear up arrogantly, undermining with its smile the image of a wait only founded on remembrances. Every bend led you off the path, every path diverted your steps from the main road, and it was not in my honor that you were earning fame; other arms were seducing you in an embrace that weakened me, polluted me with anguish, and my struggle not to give in, to maintain the harmonious trot of rider and steed exhausted the effort, so barely realizing it, one dropped the bridle and the other slowed its pace down. The Suitors' impudence exceeded all limits and I ended up confining myself to this room... Nowadays, for me, the ropes of the bridge have been cut loose, the afternoons' purple strips me naked, the flowering of the apple trees are an unbearable shedding, the children's games sharpen the certainty of my foregone future, the scents in the streets stir in my mouth the flavor of your absence. If before my whole being fervidly anticipated our re-encounter and dared to ask for it as a divine favor, if my waiting was the crucible to which death thought itself invited, how did it come to pass that the signs were so out of kilter, that light turned into darkness and what used to be high fell to the depths and never rose up again? And if you were about to arrive today, what could I possibly offer you? Would I be able to reverse the powerlessness of my limbs, or awaken what has now turned into a gravestone? When you come back to me, my skin will interpose a rough stubble to your caress; if you call, your voice will drown in the abyss. I don't know my own name, whose name will you call? I don't know what my face looks like; on whom will your gaze come to rest? I am not even sure I will be able to speak, to say something to rescue myself, to regroup the scattered parts of my being, undo the parenthesis of our separation—how can we know if that temporary time was not in fact the other thing, more real than what existed before? To re-trace the flow of our days, to recommence, this time with words, Eurydice's ascent, challenging the legend. Will I be able to overcome the dizzying spell of cowardice that will overtake me? What can I hold onto? Surely the best thing, the most prudent thing, would be to keep quiet, to not prolong the waiting. And I notice, horrified, that no matter how tenuously, I still vibrate, I am still waiting, senselessly, for the miracle—such shamelessness! I spent this morning trying to reproduce a beat, the beat of our lovemaking of former days, oblivious, as if frozen in a dream, and I felt a great stirring in the air, a huge commotion among the seagulls, and the dog, your dog, has not stopped barking for one second. My hands have raced so fast that the tapestry is now finished. And I am afraid, yes, that something dark is threatening to rush in, irrepressibly. I shall go mad... To be so close to what one has imagined, that reality devours itself into a sort of blindness, a detachment, not because imagination and reality coincide, but because they fight against each other, so that the imagined loses the solidity of its perfection and becomes something neutral, brutal: one must track back, one must flee or get ready to die in an avalanche of screams. If it is your coming that all of this portends, I refuse to welcome it, I refuse to tear the scar open to allow you back in. I am beside myself. How can it be that after my having embraced acceptance, you are now coming back to enslave my desire? Will my soul have to yield to the coarse proof of the passage of time, to the slander of powerlessness? And you, Ulysses, what beacons burn now in your memory? Is there anything that the passing of time has not vanquished? Is there anything that remains unspoiled in its original purity? Could it be that you are only bringing your tiredness to rest it next to me? I am trembling, startled memories keep unraveling in my heart, the storm I thought vanquished long ago is now raging, my senses have been so deceived... Flee, Penelope, the scattered, the faint-hearted, don't let disappointment strike you, don't let it trap you. You will not have what you don't have, and you will not share what you will not share; you don't belong to the world of the man who is now returning with an unknown face, with breath from strange distant places, a coarse touch, eyes with no memory. The lips calling your name do not know the code for the name you are after, luminous and constant, determined, perfect. And your arms, Ulysses, will they be able to decipher the mystery of fidelity unpolluted by absence?... Flee, Penelope, may the arms of Oceanus's daughter be the ones that receive you in their embrace...

III
Eurycleia

You asked me about those letters, Ulysses; I did not know they existed, either. Carefully ordered inside the casket, without dates and without an addressee, I saw them for the first time when you showed them to me. I am not sure you do well by trying to reconstruct what her life was like during those twenty years she spent away from you, without news, or maybe only a couple of spare and vague reports. But even so, why did she flee? Because she guessed your guile under your beggar's garments? Or did she think you were really dead? I don't know, she did not confide her doubts to me, Eurycleia, the nursemaid who spent so many nights helping her unravel the woven fabric with more care than she used to comb and braid her hair. Read them, read them carefully—you might be able to find what was concealed from the eyes of this old woman who thought she knew her so well and who felt so sure of her secrets… Yes, she used to write, I don't recall when she began doing it or how, but one by one, the papyri began to arrive, and the inkwell and the pen and the drying powders. I did not attach any importance to it, "she is copying poems"—I thought—"another yearning of hers." She would spend every dawn on them before going out to the beach, well before the buzz started in the harbor or those awakening in homes saw the daylight. Swiftly she would venture out and swiftly she would come back. Alone, yes, she would not allow me to go with her, still warm from her short and deep sleep watched over by a candle she never blew out and without ever closing her curtains, whether or not the wind blew, spring or fall. And no, I don't know if she would go to meet someone. Sometimes she would come back heavyhearted, that is true, sometimes looking like a young girl. You saw her yourself that night, proud, her hair done up, bedecked like a bride, so reserved one could have said that she was actually about to be betrothed and given in marriage... But why leave the hall before seeing who could bend your bow? Go ask Oceanus's daughter...

...and I am afraid, yes—why should I not confess it? It is a painful and deepfelt fear that forces me to stay away from you, to want to stop desiring you, a fear that this much waiting might shatter, like fine crystal, inside my chest... The bard said that your ship was headed for these shores, but how many times have we been given the same news mercilessly over and over? One could say that you take pleasure in torturing me, that you hate me, that you are avenging in me some obscure affront. Oh! Were it possible to bring back to you your mother's love so that you could forgive me! If at least you would dare to tell me outright that I have been mistaken, that I should not wait, should not call for you, that it is useless to love you because the only thing I stir inside you is the distance, and that I live inside a mirage because you are a mirage...

You think that it is from fear that we sometimes tremble in the embrace, Ulysses. The man who filled my breasts with milk did not ask me for my name even though he swore he had never felt so pleased. And I believed him, why not? The morning was beautiful, we were both alone and the day was in front of us. I cooked for him and even mended his ragged coat. He received everything as a matter of course because that is what a woman is expected to do with her womanly skills. I laid him down next to me on the sheets my mother had woven for my intended wedding. Had he stayed, he would have surely scolded me afterwards for my fervid and willing surrender. But he left at dawn, promising to return by the rainy season. My womb ripened in its pleasure, but the fruit was born withered. That is how I came into service in this house, you know that. My story is not as vulgar as you would like to think, but if we are measured with the same rod and the difference does not matter anyway, why reveal oneself? There are none so blind as those who will not see. If Penelope had other lovers, I didn't know it, although I would not hold it against her: she would have done it as a way to find you, or to find herself. She used to ask me if it was possible to keep the image of a loved one having lost the smell of proximity that emanated from his skin. Smells besieged her. She would take out your vestments from the closet and search through them for your scent, she would cover herself with them. On some nights she would walk out onto the balcony, stretch out her arms and raise her voice over the hills with her lament, for hours she would sing to herself, weep… No, it is not like she said anything in particular; she rather seemed to be lulling herself to sleep, praying and asking for forgiveness. Then she would storm back to her loom in a rage. You never received her messages? Long and narrow strips she wove on her olivewood loom, informing you about all the little things, of the flight of the migrating birds—who could have said that it was with them that she would try to flee?—of the change of seasons in the fields, the winnowing of the grain, the swelling of the springs, of your son tumbling with the dog on the floor. Of her dreams, which only revealed themselves in the delicate tufted fringes, her finishing touches, in her twining of the thin gold and silver threads so thoroughly twisted they hurt her fingers, the cry of dying cranes, the smell of stored fruit, all of them signs of love restrained.

...your absence covers me like a skin disease, purulent, impossible to puncture the pustules, nothing will rid my body of it, my grieving body, why should I not mention that, too? Are you setting your sails for my island? Like autumn clouds crossing the sky in the summer light... I need the rain to put out this fire that is consuming me, the years, so many years like the nights that you have been absent from my body... "Will you give me the light of dawn at dusk?" asks the Poet, and I respond yes, you will give it to me, you will bathe me with longing, you will sway me with the wind, I will flower with sunshine, and flocks of sheep will once again graze on my belly. I will expand myself like a cloud in the full-moon sky, free of anything that confines it, and spread myself in peaceful surrender. I have begun to think of you as someone from whom I have already taken leave, but I forgot to ask Chronos about the hour when you said goodbye... Spread over me the cloak of your love and cover me, today I want to love you with passionate abandonment, to crown your head and set upon your face caresses never proffered before, unique, on your skin, your eyelids, your lips opening up on mine, caresses wherever

your longing thirsts and your weariless forehead bends, to sink my hands in your hair and sow it with wheat and then descend, like climbing up to the summit, with expectant desire, to the chalice of your belly and shelter there the fire that will carry us both, light prisms splintering, fountains breaking their seals to ease their flow towards their own center. Spread over me the cloak of your love, today I want to love you with minute detachment...

No, Ulysses, there are things that cannot be restored with words. It would not have lasted, believe me; neither her pain nor her happiness belongs to you anymore. Your eyes kept wandering, full of other faraway lands, and she stayed too close to the remembrance and the silence. When she wove upon her loom, she would try to speed up the pace of the days, as if in the momentum of the pedal she could find the answer that her fingers kept trying to extract from the rough wool. For a man, faithfulness boils down to one petty certainty: his need for a body as an anchor, and to his mother, of course; and the woman has to lie to herself and hide inside the crack, the crack from which our womanly call for Life emanates, the voice of the Goddess heard in our spasm. That is the voice a man seeks. But do you think that for us women everything turns around a caress? We allow the evidence to betray us because we hope that through the caress you will be able to discern that other bridge, the one leading to the invisible and utmost secret—the urn where the barley grain, Ceres's purple gift, ripens—the one that no one dares to cross, so narrow it is over the deep abyss and looking like it was built so haphazardly. And we always end up being truncated. But we are larger than the ocean you traverse,

Ulysses, and more luxuriant than an oak grove even though you might settle for a ditch to navigate on, or for felling only one tree to build your shelter. Taking us for moorings, you throw your ropes, still lost in your thoughts and filled with the silence of the high seas. Our mistake is to have waited so long and to have anxiously come out to meet you as if your ship had really hastened to reach the mainland. But in fact it is being held back by one obstacle: you driving your banner in, claiming us women as property and fastening us to the shore… Swaying back and forth, Penelope traversed the whole undulating range that lovers sway between: fierce hatred of your absence and of her own self for enslaving herself to the wait; the tender song of the turtledove lulling itself with hope; desire, desire like a fruit peeled of its rind; and the rejection of that desire, of that sensuality oozing out and radiating the vibration of its delicious flesh over the Suitors' desire. And I, old Eurycleia, I too spent nights living the rumor of that desire spreading, palpitating under the deep and perfumed sky mixed up with the chirping of the crickets and the twinkling of the stars answering back… Something inside us would open up, driving us to the verge of tears, urging us to kiss another's lips, to drink up all the caresses, to hold a face in one's hands and lose oneself in a pair of eyes fixed on another pair of eyes, merging each other's gaze into a single light with the same desperation you hear in the voice of someone clamoring for help… And in truth we were sinking, pulsating from dusk on, like the evening lights you know so well, white against the cliffs reflecting the water's blue that seems to ascend from the ocean's depths towards the sinking violet-colored star. We visited the oracle. Without revealing who we were, the seer announced that your fate was not inscribed anywhere in the palm of Penelope's hand, that your life line and hers only crossed at some remote point; a brief encounter that had happened, or would happen, barely the mirage of a narcissus, Cora's fascination with the golden flowers on their tall stems, the sweet and hypnotic rapture of their exhalation… An ephemeral joy, a short-lived gift. Then the abduction, the descent into the violet sea sinking into the worlds of Oblivion, that sterile land, a desolation where the wheat does not ripen, the barley sprouts pale and dry like the hair of the insane: Demeter's curse. She did not ask any questions. Hardened, she left the site, and stunned she went on walking, staring ahead without looking down where she walked and without listening to my entreaties. At first the shock seemed to grow inside her, turning her into stone, deaf and dumb, grim. She came here and emptied the trunks with your belongings—I was hardly able to stop her from throwing them into the fire—she got rid of every trace of your presence and cut her hair short, like a widow. Standing in the port she kept scanning the horizon with an icy and sharp eagerness.

…I am trapped in the wind. I am not calling a name, I am clamoring for a presence… My thighs form a shining halo when they surround your waist and the flower grows petal by petal tightening into a knot that bursts brimming over the threshold, flooding it with splendid and delicious liquid, a line stretches out forming an arrow tensed up against the back of the bow and is then launched by successive undulating movements towards the vast expanse of pleasure, a promise flowering in the dark fertile sap… Sometimes the impact of your voice gets lost in my veins leaving my blood

permeated with light, a seashell murmurs the secret flow of spheres that resonate in my memory as your whispered words reverberate through my body... My body, a broken vessel, is clamoring for your lips to seal its cracks; far away from you it is falling apart, it is growing hollow without dawn or twilight... Those afternoons when you took me in your arms, the swallows circling, bidding their farewell to the daylight and enjoying its last glimmers, where did those afternoons go, those afternoons we amassed, those special afternoons forever unique? Afternoons whose footprints step over the silence and burst into the solitude of other faceless afternoons, indistinct afternoons without your presence, is it there where they will end up, there, in the emptiness of time where, being absent, your body does not gather me up in its embrace?

There were those who approached her sincerely moved by her mourning, and not only for the promise that her likely widowhood implied. Yes, Ulysses, she was loved too, and without the bait of recompense. Not every surrender ends in a simple exhausted caress. Not every wait is a reencounter of solitude. There were those who re-created Penelope with their gaze and found her and forcibly brought her back to life. There were those who drew her out and shook her out of her stupor, and poured a trickle of sweet water on her thirst for the sea...

...you are not in a rush because you think that Ithaca is just there, sleepy under her wait. What do you know about faithfulness? Do you think that just because my body has not penetrated another body, I devoutly belong to you, a man who knows only one weapon to possess someone? What do you know about my dreams, about their secret flights? I don't depend on

your semen to wet my womb, or on your saliva to awaken my breasts. I can still stand up and shout "I don't want to," my body is sick of the burning marks of your abandonment, why wait anymore? Another's caress could still harvest my affections, another's arms could hold me, other breezes could swell the sails of my yearning for sweetness. What God would take pleasure in the feeble footprint I would leave behind by passing through this world as the widow of a living warrior? I can still stand up and shout "I don't want to;" impelled by love I can hate you and not forgive you for having let me go, so engrossed in yourself, like someone letting dust escape from between his fingers. I care less about you resting your head on someone else's breast than about the waste of my own breasts, the useless spilling of their warmth on the night's void and my pitiful efforts to rescue myself every morning. I hate the flippancy with which you abandoned me to your absence day after day, as if that absence were my true lover. I must know when this waiting will be over to decide whether to deepen my hatred or allow it to dissolve in the joy of existence, the precarious joy of a bird enjoying its freedom while imprisoned by the sky. I hate the everyday sob in my throat, the flapping of broken wings; will you never know that in my dreams I killed the messenger of your farewell? I thought that the burning embers of my love would light an echo in you and that you would stop fleeing… I want to break the waves with my feet, full of joy, and to wet my lips with my yearning for the sea, to forget the somber harvest of my merciless vigils. I want, yes, I want to swell up with ennobled seed, and for a red poppy to shine in my hair, to dance with reverent joy at the celebrations of life, and to leave behind, guilt-free, the privations I suffered for your meandering, my constant spying on your wanderings and feeling like I was part of it, like some crazy Cassandra, a phantom of myself. To forget your sirens and my weaving, the decrees of the gods and their obscure designs, the calculations of the stars… Should it happen that you come to me, do not hand me your abandonment; offer me your willing nearness tempered by your desire to possess each moment of the time of our encounter thoroughly and fully. Do not immerse our bodies in slumber if it is just a brief embrace that holds us together on a temporary bed. Open up the horizon for me, take me aboard your ship, tie me up with delicate threads of tenderness and take me, stream of live water, fruit, fire, and stretch your arms so that I come to you at the dawn of spring…

Yes, Ulysses, you would have arrived engrossed in your adventures to recount them slowly, step by step. You did not return for the embrace; you came back and you got rid of the Suitors in order to take shelter, as the only inhabitant, in the womb where you were forged. Did you ever stop to think about Penelope's face, of the traces that your time of restlessness etched on it? Waiting for you here was someone who had become a stranger, one who, far from having taken a lover, had filled up and emptied herself out in absolute loneliness. You do not even know what she took from you and what she left you, so it is you who ended up as the truly dispossessed one, you are the abandoned one, Ulysses, the deserted one. She decided to turn her waiting into an ocean to sail on, her sails swelled by their own winds. She sailed away, shortly after you arrived, in search of the same islands that held you back for twenty years, Ulysses, twenty years since you sailed for Troy…

IV
Ulysses

To me our farewell was not a separation or a departure. Saying goodbye meant keeping death away, challenging it, minimizing it, getting rid of it because it gets rid of itself. To say goodbye, the poets proclaim, is the firmest foothold, the uppermost measure of one's resistance to separation. Does a goodbye ever end? I had no reason to doubt her faithfulness, or to fear oblivion: we had built a bridge we would know how to cross from one side to the other over the river of absence—was not our bed carved from the very heart of the olive tree, and the walls of our dwelling sculpted around it as a symbol of our indissoluble union? We were woven into each other's fabric. What fear could there be if between Penelope and Ulysses everything was fair and reciprocal, our motivations and passions parallel, the space to dream shared and shared alike, and our wings were never a burden? What we offered to each other could not be touched by any hand or spoken of with possession; our face was one face, our body one body, unique, infinite, godly. Each of our encounters were new nuptials, the same sacred and savage happiness, one and the same throbbing of life being lived... You don't play with remembrances, Eurycleia, otherwise you risk being blinded by hubris and arousing the Gods' envy. Why should I now thresh out what our days of love were like? Do words exist to describe the indescribable? My soul was filled with that vision, what other vision could ever occupy what was already occupied? What other gaze? What other name? I never stopped thinking of her. No hiatus was possible. And I am certain that it was not news what we expected from each other: the measure of her need was the measure of my need. There was no need to add anything, we knew that only two virginal brows could crown each other with fidelity and purity... You reproach me, Nurse, for not having remained faithful because I gave in to the embrace of another's arms and reclined my head on another breast, but I did not think I would lose her body in my contact with other bodies until I felt that she might have lost mine, her waist encircled by other arms. That is when going back became urgent... You say that it was my hurt pride and not love that impelled me. But that is not fair. We men keep our eyes fixed on the horizon because we know that we are tied to the shore by a thin thread that allows us to get farther and farther away. It is not true that we only know how to pull away from what we love, forever in search of a duty to fulfill, always seeking to overcome our limits. Woman keeps pushing us on to become full men—is it not through his contact with the Mother that the Titan recovers his strength? And yet, at the last moment, driven by a dark impulse, She tries to hold us back and clip our wings in order to protect us once again. She gives us life and She gives us death with equal passion. Woman lives love through the hearth and attaches to it a magical certitude. To us, love is conquest, to come out of the labyrinth and confront the Minotaur. But in that face-to-face encounter, love fades away: it is our own voice that we hear, our own defenseless fear, our vulnerable loneliness that we have to vanquish alone by ourselves, without filters or threads, taking measure of our own selves all the way to victory. Earth does not give generously unless you have previously tilled her fields; she does not offer her gifts unless you have offered yours first to her, forever thirsty, forever triumphant. A strange exchange not ordained by Heaven… We are the sons and husbands of the Mother in whose womb we consummate our possession, birth and death. That is why, Eurycleia, there is no possibility of comradeship between man and woman, none whatsoever, Nurse, none… Circe, the sorceress, gave me everything and would not allow me to give her anything in return. Filling me up to the brim, she would smother me with her gifts, leaving me useless, annihilated. What could I give to her? That is how they subdue us men, and get hold of our courage, weakening us like suckling infants. Calypso, on the other hand, spied on me, her solicitude was like a tireless eye. Every one of my movements, gestures. Even when she pretended to be busy at her tasks, and while I roamed the island; even at leisure, in my dreams I felt like a prisoner… Are you saying that deep down I liked that prison because in the end I was master of her body and could indulge my lust? I do not know, sometimes I felt like a madman longing for his own soul. I felt used. She did not love me for who I was and for what I could offer her. Her demands were incomprehensible, nothing made her happy, she wanted to hear herself talk and for me to just listen to her. My own dreams upset her, and if it was me who became impatient she would trick me into recounting my adventures, the ones that demanded most of my strength; that is how she would corner me in the immediate past, concretely in that interval where those feats were pure present tense, action, combat, right there where all of us become oblivious to our bonds and yearnings; and I succumbed... You are right, Eurycleia, vanity sinks us men; we need the mirror that Woman swings back and forth before our eyes to praise us and aggrandize us like gods and receive homage. At times, it was not I but she who recounted my feats, embellishing them, although frankly, her ability to reproduce the spectacle fascinated me, it was not for nothing the Olympians praised her skill so. Yet, even on those occasions she would not excel for my sake, but for hers, to show her power and to captivate me, and I hated her tricks and my capacity to lie, and I sought to humiliate her, yes, for there is no closer bond than that game of mutual degradation and mutual reproach, a game of spite that kept our minds working, sharpening our wits to turn trifles into gigantic accusations that would end up stimulating the pendulum towards reconciliation. Because we also obeyed our bodies' call for pleasure, I do not deny it, the exhalations of pure obedience, unrestricted, faithful only to its needs and pleasure, taking from desire its joy and its coltish frenzy, offering with a caress its unrepressed love, exploding vertigos, unmistakable complicity of two rivals yielding to each other in the same clash of spasms, winners and losers, unparalleled truce where blood and breath rest after the contest as only one shield and only one spear... For seven years I remained, spellbound; your reprimand is fair, Nurse, seven years enslaved to that powerful temptation named Happiness, being rocked like an immortal, free of pain amidst pleasure's contentments, dazed by the purring of its half-finished sentences, blinded by its titillating vibrant sparks... But as time passed I began to allow silence to write in my heart so I could hear the voices from afar, the voices of my hearth and of my son, the voices of my land, your voice, Nurse, the shade of the olive trees, the vineyards. With what words could I describe to you how my yearning began to seep into me, turning into a small pebble coursing through my veins? Fate does not come calling only once in a lifetime, but how often are we able to hear, follow, obey its call? Do we know clearly what we need? We are but a fleeting shadow, a fantastic illusion, like sleepwalkers we spin around what dazzles us and think ourselves masters of the blind forces that trouble us. And yes, the lips of the wound inflicted by absence, those lips that I kept shut by means of sheer courage, opened up everywhere in my body, and I ended up feeling expelled from the world and from everything, and I woke up to the possibility of never being able to hold Penelope in my arms again, and that was one more heartache, a deep and numbing fright beyond tears and screams, a bewilderment, a drunkard's stupor, a tremor inside me as if my entrails had come loose, a present-time sorrow for past and future absences, the pain of empty hands... I was not prepared to envision absence, Nurse. During the siege of Troy my mind lived in the ordinariness of a cold war and the trifles of the encampment's activities to train and distract us from the useless pent-up tensions, my life spent in the games, the petty intrigues, the rites to propitiate the Gods, the schemes to crush the city and its inhabitants. Our rush to put an end to our waiting also numbed us to the passage of time, for something new would always happen to distract the impatience of those of us looking forward to a future that felt so near that we wanted to touch it; ours was a fever for either death or victory... The other kind of waiting I only experienced when I started out on the road back home, at the mercy of my doubts and the whims of destiny. I ceased being a hero and became a man returning home, tied down from afar by Penelope's waiting, and more immediately by the traps the Gods laid in my way. That is when I learned the meaning of the possible, and to play with what could have happened during my absence. You will say that I woke up too late and at the wrong time, Eurycleia, and that is true. You believe that I could have easily extricated myself from the spells, from the delay; that ten years in the service of a war that today seems unfair and useless was enough to make me reflect and experience the numbing and raging desperation that distant bodies longing for each other suffer, and you reproach me for having lost ten more years without protesting the arbitrariness of the Gods who punished and tested my hero's conceit by hindering my return home and thrusting me instead into the excitement of danger and adventure. For it is true, I will not deny the excitement of overcoming one obstacle after another, of the constant measuring of my guile against the cruel and brute forces of nature unleashed or against beings like the lotus-eaters and the Cyclops, or of competing with men and demigods as part of my search for new experiences and knowledge; the excitement of the struggle of the will to tame the limitations and weaknesses of a frightened heart, the same will that according to you, Eurycleia, saved me from the siren's song but not from the temptation to abandon myself to love's contentments, the mirage of that fleeting moment I would like to squeeze like sweet nectar between my lips… Ah, Nurse! We were created to love beauty, to contemplate the peaceful surface of its stillness and to lose ourselves in it, for beauty is a poppy plant… "Search for me in the impossibility of containing me," our longing for the infinite tells us. You should spend an entire night under the skies in the middle of the ocean to understand how your soul gradually fills up with that voice that projects you so far back and so far ahead in time that you lose your memories and desires and you expand beyond them into that dimension where all questions and all unfulfilled dreams are allowed, beyond the existence of the Gods themselves, past their fights and their continuous meddling in ours, purified of martial vindictiveness, however exalting and glorifying that vital impulse might be. There, on the ocean you are not your own self anymore, but the self of worlds unknown, a brother of the star, radiance of its radiance, silent palpitation, and so eloquent, Nurse, so palpable… What was there in the beginning and how did things come to be? What prior Order governs the order of the universe and the order of the Gods? Human greatness can be brought down in one day and in one day built up again, what then does our passing through this world mean? The shades of the dead I evoked around the blood of the sacrifice at the entrance of Hades were but a dread of emptiness, a longing for the vital breath and the radiant sun. I felt pity and compassion for the void of the oblivion in which they wandered. A pale fright took hold of me when I realized that at some point in time I would become part of that procession, and that I had already rejected immortality from the hands of the Nymph and the Magician… What is the life of a mortal?

It is a search bound by implacable reasons. This was the self I was assigned to be, Eurycleia, the hero, sly, dodgy, tireless, and I wanted to fulfill that role all the way to the end. But one is never the same after having killed one's peer, a transient creature like oneself, and one is never the same after having experienced the cruelty with which Fate confuses our will and our understanding. I shall never forgive myself for the madness that afflicted Ajax because of me, and I shall forever admire the courage of his rebelliousness against adversity and against the force of Hades: it was not the Fates that snatched him away at the end of his prescribed days, he snatched his own life away, fully aware of his decision... And what is the grief of a mortal?... No, Eurycleia, I was not prepared to envision her absence... "Gods," I used to pray, "grant me water for my keel and wind for my sails, I want to set off, quickly, towards our reunion." And what did I get but the unleashing of Oceanus's fury? Yes, I was a tired man eager to see the smoke of my native land, and it is true, I acknowledge, that my yearning to leave also grew because the Nymph did not please me anymore, and that afterwards, in spite of my longing, Circe's amorous snares further entangled and twisted my steps back home. I knew that Ithaca waited faithfully for my return, Penelope's embrace included, it was that certainty that gave me courage and strengthened my spirit... It was a one-sided comfort you will say, because I did not think of her waiting, of her vigil, her wasted dreams. But that is not entirely so; how would I have otherwise been able to vanquish the Fates' obstacles and animosity if not for having experienced the security of our home, the solidity of its walls and the warmth that Penelope kept between them? The smallest hesitation, the smallest doubt would have instantly consumed me, just like my flesh began to burn with that insidious feeling of "never again," my hands longing for her narrow waist. Penelope's unchanging presence occupied a space inside me that brimmed, unbounded, to the top. There was no reason to compare her with anyone because no other face could have altered the image I kept of her in my mind's eye, no other fire quenched the serene flame that kept burning, unaffected by distance, at the center of all my acts, like a compass, a lighthouse… And today you tell me, Nurse, that Penelope has left, and you turn over to me some papers you say she wrote during my absence. I did not repair my bow to meet the Unexpected, or vanquish the Suitors only for the sake of pent-up jealousy. I am here because Penelope has been the guardian of my roots. Can the sower just hand over his seed without depositing it in the furrow that will fertilize it? I am the one who came in order to be called by my name by her, the one returning from his wandering days back home, the father of my son and her son's father, the one who has come to catch his breath again, the fugitive who did not fear to cross the night sheltered by the hope of dawn, a naked man entering the sanctuary to be purified… Where shall the harvest I am carrying on my back be reaped, and who will share with me the baked bread? Whose voice will reply to the voices that I have brought from afar, impatiently waiting to be born? Whose ears will free the captive word sunk in the silent sorrow in which her silence has left me?... Ah! Implacable justice! I understand, incorruptible Tyche, the part of the harvest that has been justly allotted to me: "woe to whoever arrives too late, like a beggar, he shall find every door closed to him"… The sun and the moon cling to the sky; the grain and the trees get their sustenance from the earth, but what can my soul hold on to in order to keep shining? Oh, Eurycleia! Penelope has abandoned me to the mercy of Time…

V
Epilogue

When the messenger delivers this letter to you, Ulysses, I will have set off towards the Island of Everlasting Time. I know you are not going to look for me, that is why I am not hiding my destination. But before entering that sacred place, I want to speak with you, to break my silence all the better to savor it later on there, where only those who have purified their memory from their bitter grudges and obsessive nostalgia can enter. I did not know that by fleeing I would be sailing towards you, and that I would somehow end up waiting here, too, waiting for an arrival that time keeps delaying and which, engrossed, I keep weaving exactly as I have woven myself. There is one difference, however. Here there is not even a trace of you so I am free to invent everything—I left so many remembrances tied to my loom, so many loose threads— beginning with my own destiny. I do not claim that the Gods gave me one different from what I would have chosen for myself. I am what I might have vaguely hoped to be, for what we are is tightly, inseparably sewn to our actions. That this being may remain forever curled up in itself is possible. But it will suffice to pull, however lightly, the thread at one end for the spool to begin unraveling and for our features to start blurring, fading slowly, irreversibly falling away. It is the real that we shall never know how to capture, express… But I am not writing to you assailed by a rush of nostalgia. Like Deianeira, I might be weaving the last tunic you wear on your shoulders. Although not precisely out of spite… Penelope is no more, she has been left behind. The person now speaking to you does not care by what name she is called: Cora, Circe, Nobody. Was that not what you named yourself? Although in my case it is not motivated by a desire to conceal anything. Neither my memories nor my dreams matter anymore. I am not trying to stir your soul, or to request, or to ask. I only want to resume my scream, pulling it up by its very roots and climbing with it the ramparts of Time, its hard core, for what purpose is there in offering my soul to the Gods if it is torn apart?

…it is difficult to know where anguish ends and faith begins, says the Poet. And yes, the days are a web of trivial miseries, slanted, whiny, yet how powerfully could the fullness of an embrace rescue them, one ecstasy, a light. And I will not deny those afternoons with your head lying on my knees, or when intertwined, our bodies rested from their embrace exhaling their reveries, pouring them out like fountains into a crepuscular pond. The most difficult thing, Ulysses, was to accept a clear and simple fact: that you stopped loving me, that you began to forget me, to feel comfortable with the absence, like lying on a secure and soft bed… Ulysses, that immutable absent presence painfully coming unstrung inside the scar of my memory.

Ulysses of the thousand names, a stranger even to his own self... There are more silent sorrows than the sorrow of weaving, I know that. Maybe yours was one of those: silent, mute in the muteness of what one has resolved to keep silent, to keep even its silence silent. But grief is bad. It does not liberate. It does not purify. Instead it pollutes, it desecrates life, rotting its bright and spontaneous happiness... Silencing happiness. Nothing is as frightening as to give up the joy of living and to confine it to silence... To give up one's own self in favor of guilt.

I am not sure I did not behave recklessly by leaving. I wonder if reason always dictates our acts, if we are able to explain what exactly impels us in those moments when our being is struggling to darkly break through the darkness, to narrowly break off its narrowness. What arguments could one use to do away with that itchy wool suffocating one's breast and blurring one's eyesight? There aren't any. There is only the violent reaction of vomiting and clearing one's eyes... I cannot claim that it was the accumulated rage in my gut, or my desire to vindicate my sleeplessness, or the emptiness caused by your absence that pushed me into abandoning the shuttle and the baking stone. Neither should you think that I was I bored with them. Nor was it out of spiteful envy to imitate your exploits that I abandoned the warmth of the ovens and the monotonous eurythmy of the domestic chores, or the babbling and the hustle and bustle of the threshing, grinding, sifting, carding, bleaching, or the agitated frolic of the maidens oblivious to the men spying on them, their arms naked, barefoot, breasts exposed, joyfully splashing in the ditches, or the irksome caring for my son, the willful, hermetic, implacable witness of my solitude, the same solitude that I still carry glued to my skin, smooth, soft, splashed by the sun and scoured by the sea. No. It happened one night. The garden was damp, it had rained hard. I was listening to the sound of the snails crawling on the stones. And I felt the touch of the call, Ulysses, a call that did not resemble, no, not at all, the call of the sirens, for it did not come from the outside or demand an immediate answer. It was rather like a longing for something to open up, for the horizon to widen to the limit of its deep heartbeat, and for expanding one's voice, one's face, one's gaze toward dawns never before tread on by sadness; a longing for a sense of immense lightness in one's arms, for a space inside one's belly, a longing so deep and wild, lips flowing, a fullness in the fingers, an anticipated joy of traveling... A call, Ulysses, akin to the movement of the wheat stalks in the air, and the undulation of the anemones in the deep sea, pale, self-absorbed; to the loosening, soft and slow, very slow, of the seaweed that used to anchor my sighs to the rock of your absence.

...desire has been leaving me, sinking in its own intensity... Would it have helped me any to say I do not want to desire you anymore? Today I want to immerse myself in the sea of forgiveness, I want to beg for mercy for the crumb of resentful salt lodged in my heart that sometimes leaves a bitter taste in my mouth... It is no longer my yearning burning me up, or my deep rage for your long absence... It is not the body distanced from the other body that is calling, it is the bared soul of your voice that is screaming...

…I dreamt of a river of white water, with it I kept washing my face until it shone. I did not see when the stain appeared, I was so absorbed combing my hair. Trying to wash it out, I cried a little and I carefully rubbed it. When it turned red, I thought it would disappear into a wrinkle in my skin. But it became embedded inside me. So, like King Midas, I tried to hide the secret in the heart of a reed. The anguish this caused me set off blasts of hail in my bones…. The time when you said goodbye: why did I want to know it? Was it not always there, from the beginning, a guest of the hours we stole away from Time, a mirror of our embraces and our words, a shade in your distant gaze? You let me go from your dreams, distracted, you abandoned me like a broken-up dinghy consigned to oblivion; my body was weighing you down and you did not want to support it anymore. You were in a hurry to return to the elation of your fighting. Sleepwalker, what will happen to you without the testimony of my presence, to you, an exile? And I?... Do I exist? I have come to ask myself. Absent from your gaze, without your hands on my face, do I exist? For how long?...

You will forget me, Ulysses, I know that. You are forgetting me already, burying me in your memory… It's easier that way, to numb the insatiable yearning for a presence, and to avoid crying out like the vast, infinite burnt-out desert does by imbibing its own mirages… You will forget, without the sea, the island, your boat, until your bones become liquid and your memories salt, until your yearning disappears and you are able to get up one morning free of that insatiable thirst… I thought myself strong, Ulysses, ready to take flight, but I was wrong…

You will say that it is out of pride that I have not returned. But I am only being consistent. I did not have your support. The solidity of our four walls could not give that to me, nor could the waiting, nor could our son. I wonder if you will ever understand what I was asking from you… There were times when I tried to forget you. I did try. Just like you will. In those days your image faded from my mind like a hill crumbling in the slow persistent waters; enormous boulders would slide to the center of my breast, smothering my memory of you. There were no tears in those days. Only stupor. A vise pressing on my temples, charred skin on my flesh. Nothing could have rescued me in those days. And I would not have been able to recognize you, my eyes had fallen back into their own sockets… But forgetting takes a long time, it takes a long time for the creases and cracks to disappear from a body with an enormous glowing scar irrevocably opened by a presence… We speak with wounded words, Ulysses, we fill them with reasons we are not able to understand, and we grab on to any glimmer of logic to avoid going crazy… So, in order to understand you, to avoid devouring with hatred what in fact we lived to its fullest, I decided to set off and retrace your steps, to follow the course of your adventures and relive the hurdles of your return… I wanted to go in search of my own waiting… Calypso, divine among the Goddesses, the nymph with the lovely tresses, knew of my arrival and my crazy designs. It was not necessary to go any farther. There, we experienced everything, the unique radiance of your presence in each of her evocations of your exploits, the anxiety of your shipwrecks, the eagerness that drove your search… Ulysses, Ulysses, I am burning, I am burning the remnants of my pain in this writing journey…and I want to finish this once and for all… Calypso displayed for me all your transformations, and out of love for my love, she re-lived with me her embraces with you. It was something unlike anything else, warm like a kiss but more humid, close like a hug but closer. It was an unraveling slow swirl that started in my belly and stopped abruptly in my throat. Lying on the hay, I felt happiness swelling, everything was quivering as if touched by invisible fingernails. The rays of the sun were undressing us little by little. All around was light, and I was trembling. My eyelids, my arms, my legs took possession of you, and we became one with the breeze blowing through the hay. That is when I realized that I wanted to penetrate you, yes, to wound you in each caress with the same jagged glass you used to wound my being. But not to fuse with you. No. To penetrate you instead, and then to get out; to penetrate you and leave inside you a burning arrow, to make you feel the center of my center with its tip. To explode your being from the inside of your being, and to liberate it, freeing my own self from the jail I built for myself inside you…

…I shall have to rearrange everything. Not in order to stamp out the memory of my yearning, of our rainy afternoons, the rose tea, or anything else. No. Just to rearrange things. The solitude, the silence, some stubborn memories. Gather it all; don't allow it to float wildly, don't let it get entangled in my fingers and cut them with its sharp edge… The silence—tell me Ulysses—does it speak? What does silence say when it is silent?…

About the Contributors

Esther Seligson (1941-2010) was a Mexican writer, poet, playwright, essayist, translator, and academic. She was born in Mexico City in 1941, to Jewish immigrants from Eastern Europe. She graduated from the Autonomous University of Mexico (UNAM), where she studied Spanish and French Literature. Deeply interested in philosophy, mythology, and religions, she left Mexico to study at the Sorbonne and the University of Bordeaux, and later at the University Center of Jewish Studies in Paris and the Pardes Institute of Jewish Studies in Jerusalem. Moved by those same interests—"passions" as she called them—she also stayed for extended periods of time in Southern India, Lisbon, Toledo, and Prague. She translated several French philosophers and writers who deeply influenced her life-long work, including Emil M. Cioran and Edmond Jabes. Her novel *Otros son los sueños* (*Different Dreams*) won the Xavier Villaurrutia Prize in 1973. *Luz de dos* (*The Light Inside Us*), a collection of short stories, earned the Magda Donato Prize in 1979. Among her other works are *La morada en el tiempo* (*Dwelling in Time*), 1981; two poetry books *Simiente* (*Seed*), 2004, and *Negro es su Rostro* (*Thou Who Are Dark of Hue*), posthumously published in 2010; and *Todo aquí es polvo* (*Everything is Dust Here*), also released posthumously in 2010.

Selma Marks, translator, was born and raised in Mexico City. She lives in New York City where she has worked as an interpreter for over fifteen years. She has translated plays and fiction, mostly by

Mexican authors. One of those translations, *Nobody Saw Them Leave*, by Eduardo Antonio Parra, was published in *Review: Literature and Arts of the Americas*, Issue 96, Vol. 51, Number 1, June 2018.

Naomi Lindstrom is Gale Family Foundation Professor in Jewish Arts and Culture and Professor of Spanish and Portuguese at the University of Texas at Austin. She has translated Roberto Arlt's novel, *The Seven Madmen* (River Boat Press, 2018) and has published extensive literary criticism, including *Early Spanish American Narrative* (University of Texas Press, 2004).

Read more from Frayed Edge Press...

Literature

Right Guy, Wrong Time: A #MeToo Love Story by Louise MacGregor
The Ghettobirds poetry by Bryant O'Hara
Ambushing the Void short stories by James McAdams
*¿Cómo Hacer Preguntas? or How To Make Questions: 69 Instructional
    Poems (in English)* by Daniel Hales
Bellapalma by Jens Bjørneboe; translated by Esther Greenleaf Mürer
Ere the Cock Crows by Jens Bjørneboe; translated and with a
    reconstruction of the play by Esther Greenleaf Mürer
Stealing: A Novel in Dreams by Shelly Brivic
The Splooge Factory poety by Christina Springer

History and Politics

Jeremiah Hacker: Journalist, Anarchist, Abolitionist by Rebecca
    Pritchard
A Nurse's Story: Medical Missionary in Korea and Siberia, 1915-1920
    by Delia Battles Lewis
*"Do Not Misunderstand Me": The Collected Radical Addresses to the
    Unity Congregation (1888-1891)* by Hugh Owen Pentecost

Street Smart Series - Short Fiction for People on the Go

Full Fare by Jean-Bernard Pouy
Down and Out in Paris, with Cat by R.A. Bolo
The Accidental Anarchist by A.R. Melnik
Stealing MacGuffin by Matthew Kastel
Pele's Domain by Albert Tucher

Visit us at: https://www.frayededgepress.com/